The Beach Of Secrets

A Gripping And Bloodcurdling Mystery

By: JJ Krupitzer

Table of contents:

Intro

July 19, 1982, a three-year-old boy by the name of Quincy Anderson was on vacation with his family. He was on vacation with his family in Crystal River Florida, innocently digging a Sandcastle. As he was digging with his little blue shovel, he found a bone. He ran over to his mother and said; "look mama, doggy food!" His mother, Margaret who shouted in horror, "that is not dog food Quincy, put that down right now!" His father David asked him where he found the bone and he pointed his father in the direction of which he found it. He led his father by the hand where they continued to dig. After they dug for a while, they discovered the rest of the human remains. Quincy, being three years old, started to freak out. His father eventually called The police and they took the bones for examination. Follow Quincy and his family on this monstrous journey, there will be twists and turns so stay tuned in!

Chapter 1: Howdy Peeps

Hello everyone, Allow me to introduce myself, My name is David Alexander Anderson. Born December 25, 1953, born in Amarillo Texas but raised in Pittsburgh Pennsylvania. So, I guess you could call me a southern but not so southern born dude. My parents were Marla and Martin Anderson of Dallas Texas. My parents weren't exactly poor, but we weren't exactly rubbing elbows with the elite. My mother was a well-known seamstress in Amarillo and my dad was the head coach of the Amarillo Argonauts college football team. I was two months premature, or so I was told by my mother. After a brief stint with the Amarillo Argonauts, my father was fired for bogus allegations of sexual harassment with young cheerleaders. Even though it was proven that he did nothing wrong, the Argonauts would not admit their mistake and made the firing stand!

After being shamed out of Amarillo, we moved to Pittsburgh Pennsylvania when I was just four months old. Somehow, someway I still developed the Texan accent, I really don't know how though. This was considering the fact that I had only known Pittsburgh as my home. I was too young when we moved from Amarillo to develop any behaviors of a Texan. My mother opened up her own seamstress shop on Brookline Boulevard, in Pittsburgh's Dormont neighborhood. The first couple months of living in Pittsburgh, business for my mother was slow and nobody at this time would hire my father because they Heard the rumors of my dad being a pervert. Even though they were unfounded and untrue, my mother understood why everyone was apprehensive to hire him.

"Marty, We have to figure out something, I can't be the only one working!" He was sipping a beer and he put it down and he started shouting at my mother. "I know that Margaret I know that, don't you think I know that? Why don't you stop being a bitch and get the fuck off my back?!" It was then that I heard a loud quack from my father's hand against the skin of my mom's face. This was when I was about 2 years old so my dad had no luck finding jobs from my four months of life up until my two years of life. He quickly apologized to my mother for slapping her, but she threatened to call Pittsburgh police. My father begged and pleaded with her not to call the police, and she agreed so long as she never struck her again. She promised to never do it again and they made up pretty quickly after that. My dad got his big break as an automobile salesman in the middle of 1955.

David's auto stop was run by David Capelli A lovely and what I thought to be older Italian gentleman who decided to give my dad a second chance despite hearing the rumors of what happened in Amarillo. He had a beautiful daughter by the name of Francesca who my dad was going all gaga over. Francesca Capelli, age 19, Francesca stood about 5'2" tall and had pretty but short red hair. Of course the red hair was not natural, because it was like fire engine red. Every time she would go past him, you could feel my father drooling over her. My mother didn't like this and urged him to quit his job. "Quit, quit?! You want me to quit my only job in the past two years, are you an insane woman?" My father shouted at my mother. The two of them got into a huge fight, which actually turned into a scuffle.

After the fight was over, my mother emerged from the ground with a black eye and a bloody lip. Even though she started the scuffle, she proceeded to call Pittsburgh police on my father and tell them that he had abused her. "She's lying, I didn't touch the bitch!" He said as he was being handcuffed and put in the back of a police car. Naturally because my mother was a woman, the police automatically took her side, especially back in those days. My dad spent the next nine years in prison for abusing a woman. During that time my mother was a bit of a slut. Basically bedding anyone she could find while I was growing up. I remember the first guy when I was about five years old, his name was Michael Smithers. Michael is a very nice black man, he always would take me to the park and let me play with other children. Let's keep in mind though, this is the 1950s, my mother dating a black man during that time was not looked kindly upon by the Pittsburgh community.

After being ridiculed for a couple of months for her choice, my mother decided to break it off with Mr. Smithers! The second man came into my life about age 7, his name was Dalton Masterson. Mr. Masterson actually stayed pretty consistently as I was growing. In fact, Mr. Masterson stayed in my life for about a year at age 8. The next two men were in and out of my life so quickly, I didn't even take the time to learn their names because it wasn't all that important. My mother and I would visit my father in jail on occasion. My father was always nice to me, But you could see the coldness and resentment towards my mother on his face. She did try to apologize multiple times, but my father was understandably too angry to accept her apology. "You know, this was a really random thing for you to do to me Esther, I don't think I can ever forgive you for this. My dad was released a couple years early from prison when I was nine.

After my dad's release from prison, my mother and father tried working on things desperately. They wanted to stay together for my well-being, the two of them actually got married on June 19, 1962 in Boca Raton Florida, this was somewhere that my parents always wanted to go so they figured why not get married there. I was so happy that my parents were able to reconcile and we were able to be a family again. My happiness was short-lived, as they had divorced only two years later, actually on their second anniversary, June 19, 1964. 1964 is when I became an angry child. I began getting into fights at school, and being an asshole of a child. It was so bad that my mother and father both agreed to send me to a boys finishing school so I could learn discipline and respect.

"Fuck you Dad, I am not going to a boys finishing school, you can't make me!" When I said those words, I instantly regretted them because this was the 1960s and when you mouthed off to your parents, you got belted. There was really no child protective services or anything to protect you. I tried telling my relatives about the situation, but they said I deserved it for mouthing off to my father. On July 1, 1964, they dropped me off at Robertson Academy for boys. I tried to sweet talk my way into coming home with them, but it didn't work. My mom and dad gave me a hug goodbye and hopped back in the family car and drove away. For the next six years I wrote to them nearly every week for them to come and get me. Naturally, I got no response. That is until August 1, 1970. The letter basically informed me that I couldn't come home, I couldn't come home because I wasn't a son that they raised.

I was hurt by what they had said, of course I was the son that they raised, I was just going through a tough time and they didn't understand that. Sure I was 17, but I still needed my mom and dad to stay together so that I could have stability in my life. A lot of you might say; "well that's up to you to make the stability." You would be right to tell me that, but I needed my parents approval and I wasn't getting it. After leaving the Academy, I joined the army and served from 1970 until 1972 while getting an honorable discharge for some health problems. After being discharged from the army, I went to USC to obtain a degree in childhood education. My first year at USC, that's why I met the love of my life Margaret Yakimoto. A woman of Asian dissent that caught my eye almost immediately. I was sitting in the study hall when I saw her, she had dropped her books and I was helping her pick them up. I looked into those little chinky eyes of hers and I fell in love.

We began dating later that year in 1972. Her family did not approve of me, her family wanted to have her date someone that was her "unkind" her father Yoshida Yakimoto was a very respected businessman in California, selling boats and RVs. Her mother Jin Soo Yakimoto was like my mother, a seamstress. They spoke English, but it was very broken. "You do not marry this man, he is no good for you. He bring shame to our family, you marry him, you out of family forever!" Her father barked. One night while making love, I stopped in mid pump, I looked at Margaret and I said; "you know, maybe your fathers right, maybe I'm not good enough for you." She told me to stop worrying and begin to kiss me, amongst other things. Let's just say, Margaret was very talented with her mouth (I will leave that to your imagination). Her mother and father had invited us to brunch one day and they asked Margaret about her decision. When she told her father that she still planned to marry me, Mr. Yakimoto's face turned a horrible shade of red. He was screaming something in Chinese, Japanese, Vietnamese, I don't know what it was but I know he wasn't happy.

She was saying something back to him in her native tongue, but I couldn't understand it. By the time it was over, Mr. Yakimoto and his wife had stormed out of the restaurant. I looked over and Margaret and she had been crying. I had told her that if I was going to cause this much of a rift between her and her family, I could easily depart and never talk to her again."Martin, I don't want you to do that, I want you to stay with me. Please promise me that you will never leave me?" She said with tears in her eyes. I told her that I would leave, I told her that I would always be by her side. She was finishing her doctorate at USC when I graduated in 1974. She said that she wanted to be a pediatrician, helping kids was her passion. "I know it is babe, and I know you will be a great doctor someday!" I said to her as I kissed her cheek while she was studying.

While finishing her doctorate, she got some horrible news, Margaret's dad had died. I wasn't particularly saddened by this, Mr. Yakimoto was a huge jerk to me so I didn't care if he lived or died. I feel bad for Margaret though, that was the only father she had and they stopped speaking because of me! I took the phone call and waited until she got done with school to tell her. Why didn't I tell her immediately? Well, I knew that Markett took her studies seriously and I didn't want to disrupt her mojo. Should I have told her immediately? Probably so, but I didn't want to ruin her academic prowess. When I told her about her father, she fell to her knees in sadness and regret. "My papa, my papa is gone, what am I going to do now?" She said while crying hysterically. I didn't know what to say, so I sat there and I held her until the tears stopped flowing. To be honest to the night I told her about her dad, I was horny as shit but I didn't ask her for sex because it wouldn't be appropriate for the time frame.

I didn't ask for it, but that night she gave it to me. Surprisingly she wanted to go for hours, my estimation was that she wanted to do this to get all of her emotions out. Her father died on June 7, 1972 of throat cancer. We laid him to rest on June 10 of 1972. On June 31 of the year, we found out she was pregnant. Well at least in the beginning stages. We went to her OB/GYN to check on the baby every month, everything was turning out OK at least until the third month. On September 17 of 1972, we had gotten the news that we had lost our baby. This put Margaret in a deep and spiraling depression. Even to the point that she tried to commit suicide. I told her that it wouldn't be worth it, and if we were meant to have a baby, God would provide us with another one. It wasn't for lack of trying, but we couldn't get pregnant for the next few years. During that timeline, Margaret and I tied the knot on June 17, 1973

We were madly in love, but we just couldn't get pregnant. You know between you and I, I never understood the term "we are pregnant". I'm not the one who's pregnant, my wife is, No man ever is so why do we take credit and say we're pregnant? The only thing that we do is we stick our dicks into a little tunnel and get to have fun. The woman is the one who has to carry the baby for a full nine months. But anyway I digress, we found out that Margaret was pregnant again on December 31 of 1978, we found out she was about a month along. On July 2, 1979, Quincy Derek Anderson was born. 6 pounds and 3 ounces. He was the most beautiful baby boy that I had ever seen, he had my brown hair but his mother's perfect green eyes. I didn't know if I could be a father, but once I held Quincy in my arms, I vowed to never let anyone hurt him as long as I was alive.

My parents begged me to see him. "I thought I wasn't the son that you raised." I said to my father coldly. "Son, I didn't mean what I said back then. Besides, you have turned into a fine young man. A lot better man than when you left us. " I did allow them to see Quincy, I thought about not letting them see him, but then what kind of son would I be? My mother and father picked him up and put him in their arms, they immediately said how precious he was and how proud we are of me. This made me happy inside, even though I will never really admit that to them. After a month off from her practice, Margaret had gone back to work. Since I didn't really have a job at the time, I told Margaret that I would watch Quincy while she worked. I loved being a stay at home dad, I loved getting to spend all the time in the world with my son.

Even though my wife was moderately successful, her paychecks were not enough to get us through. I knew that I had to get a job, but I couldn't bear the thought of somebody besides me or Margaret watching our son. I took a job as a car mechanic at Peterman's garage and car dealership. I doubled as a car salesman and a mechanic. So when I wasn't fixing cars I was selling them and vice versa. We found a young girl by the name of Priscilla McKinley. She was our neighbor's daughter, 14 years old and very nice. She told me that she would take care of Quincy for a very minimal payment of three dollars an hour. I tried offering her more but she said that she wasn't doing it for the money, she had a little brother of her own and she just loves watching children. I smiled and gave her a list of everything to do for Quincy. Before I left the house for work, I waved goodbye to Quincy and Priscilla and gave Quincy a kiss on the cheek.

I had sent my résumé to a couple of schools in the Pittsburgh area, but I had no bites. This being the late 1970s, we didn't really have computers or emails so I quite literally took a bunch of copies of my résumé and sent them to school districts in different states. I got a call from a school district in Stockton, California and I immediately accepted the position. Except I forgot to consider one thing, talking to Margaret about the move."You expect me to give up my business, my dream, my everything, just so we can move to California for your dreams?" She said to me in anger. I understood where she was coming from, but this was a once in a lifetime opportunity for me. I couldn't afford to pass it up!" This resulted in a huge fight and almost divorce between us, but we managed to reconcile and move to Stockton California. I could tell that Margaret wasn't happy, I could tell that she was still pissed but I was grateful that she was by my side.

Margaret opened up a second pediatric care center in Stockton. Children from all around California, not just Stockton, came to see her. Things got to the point where we had to have someone babysit Quincy all the time because we were never home. I was at work from six in the morning till about 4 o'clock in the afternoon Monday through Friday and Margaret was constantly on call. Actually, it almost caused a cosmic tear in our marriage. We were constantly At each other's throats because we felt that neither one of us was taking care of Quincy properly. The babysitter said she didn't mind looking after Quincy but that wasn't the point. The point was, we didn't want to make Quincy feel neglected. We thought by being gone all the time, Quincy would think that we didn't love him. We left him with a foreign exchange student at a nearby university, her name was Reshma Mondavi. She was about 20 years old and she took an immediate shine to Quincy, and Quincy to her.

How did we find Miss Mondavi? Well I started teaching at a junior college and she said she was looking for some extra work. I told her that I had a little boy named Quincy that needed looking after and she said she would happily do it. Reshma was a really sweet girl, sweet enough for me to cheat on my wife. That's right, one night when I came home from work I noticed Reshma taking a shower in our family home, I snuck in the shower and I drilled her. When my wife came home and found us in the shower, I didn't even try to hide it, I finished and then tried to explain. Disrespectful? Perhaps, the right thing to do? Perhaps not! Well, actually, I know it wasn't the right thing to do. Margaret had given me everything, and I just might have thrown it away for a one night fling. Why? Reshma was hot! What was I supposed to do? I am a man, I have needs, needs that my wife was not meeting at the time.

At this point I thought we were headed for divorce, but Margaret was surprisingly on board with trying to reconcile. "I will forgive you, if you fire Reshma! That's the only way that this will ever work between us again. "I agreed to fire Reshma, naturally, Reshma was not happy about this. "But Mr. Anderson, I thought what we had was special. You told me you were going to leave your wife!" I called her crazy and told her to get out of my house. She had said that she would make me pay someday but I wasn't scared. We went to marriage counseling, Dr. Harry Douglas. He said that I was wrong for cheating on my wife, and that if he had a wife like mine, he would tear that shit up every day! I stood up and cocked my arm back to punch him. Margaret grabbed my arm. "Don't you dare harm Dr. Douglas, it's your fault we are here, so shut up and listen to his words!"

I hastily sat back down, but I glared at him for the rest of the session. "Try to flirt with my wife, what's wrong with this man?!" I muttered to myself in anger. Margaret was right though, I had no one to blame but myself for why we were there. On the way home we didn't say much, it was raining so the rain on the windshield was making the traffic lights glow weirdly because of the water. It was pouring, and I mean absolutely pouring down rain. Margaret begged me to slow down because of the rain, but I told her I knew what I was doing and I didn't need to hear her tell me how to drive! Just then, a deer popped out of nowhere and I tried to hit the brakes, but because of the water, I couldn't stop. We went front-first into that poor and defenseless deer. I remained in my seat, Unfortunately, Margaret was thrown from the car.

Margaret had a broken arm, broken right leg (tibia and femur) She had injured her C4 and C5 vertebrae in her spine. She was completely paralyzed from the waist down. I felt regret more than I could ever express. If I would've just listened to her and slowed down, she would be healthy. Doctor's said that she may never walk again. As a matter of fact, they were almost certain of it. Margaret went into a deep depression and constantly blamed me for her being paralyzed now."OK Margaret, OK! You don't think I live with regret every day about the accident? Listen, you can make the best of the situation or you could be a whiny little bitch about it like you are being right now! The choice is yours!" She sat there with her mouth wide open, she couldn't believe that I had said something like that to her."You're so insensitive David, it's only because of you that I am like this."

I wanted to take her to physical therapy so that she could be better again, but she refused. "Margaret, you have to stop this pity party! Either you do physical therapy to make yourself better or I'm going to get a divorce. I don't wanna do that to you and I don't want to take Quincy away from you, but if I must do that then I'm going to." I said to her without hesitation. The car crash happened sometime in 1980, it took us two years for her to get remotely back into the shape that she was. She was never 100% after the accident but she improved massively. Her mother had come to visit with us while Margaret was in recovery. Her mother was no longer the better woman that I met, but yet a beacon of sunshine and laughter. She gave me a hug when she entered the home. She stayed with us until June 2, 1982 to help me take care of my ailing wife.

"I'm glad you have a good husband. Sorry that your father and I didn't like him when we first met him. He is a wonderful human being and we shouldn't have good service so quickly. I'm sure your father would agree if he was still here." She said to Margaret one night while we were getting her in bed. She gave her mother a hug. "Mama I knew you would like him, I just knew you would!" To celebrate, we agreed to go on a vacation to Crystal River Florida. When I told Quincy that we were going, he jumped up and down with excitement. He loved the idea of playing in the sand, even though he's never played in the sand before. I know we lived in California, but we never went to the beach, because we never had the time. But with my wife walking again, we decided to live each moment like it was our last. We arrived at Ft. Island Gulf Beach on July 19, 1982 at around 7 AM, we then checked into our hotel and went up to bed for a couple more hours. Quincy woke us up with excitement. "Mommy, daddy, play in the sand, play in the sand!"

We groaned because we wanted to sleep more, But we knew that Quincy wouldn't want to wait any longer. So with that being said, we pushed ourselves to get out of bed and head to the beach. It was a lovely morning, and the sun was shining, it was about 86°, without a cloud in the sky. I got dressed in my bathing suit, and I watched with glee as Margaret changed into her bathing suit. "Babe, stop staring! Especially in front of Quincy." She said as she shut the bathroom door. I waited for Margaret for what had seemed like an eternity, I'm not on the bathroom door to see if she was ready."Give me a minute babe, I'm trying to get sexy for you. When she emerged from the bathroom, my horniness turned into anger. She looks like a French whore. "What the hell are you wearing? There's no way you are going to the beach dressed like that! No wife of mine would ever go to the beach dressed like that!"

Her boobs were puffed out, her bathing suit was too tight against her skin, She looked like a clown with how much mascara she had on."Who are you getting dolled up for like that? Is there another man that you have in this state?" to which she replied; "excuse me, I can wear whatever the damn hell I want, you don't own me and I am not your property." we looked over, Quincy looked scared. "Why are mommy and daddy fighting?" We looked at him and then we looked at each other, we quickly realized that we shouldn't fight, especially around him. We are married and we are in for the long-haul, so we need to learn to coexist and cooperate with each other. we quickly kissed and said to Quincy; "mommy and daddy are not fighting, we just have disagreements sometimes. We love you very much, we are very sorry that we scared you!

As I said before, it was a beautiful day and after our fight, we spent the next couple of hours Laying together on a blanket. Then for more comfort, Margaret transferred to a chair. I was watching my son build some sand castles for about an hour and I had fallen asleep. I woke up to Margaret freaking out, I had woken up to my son holding a bone. However, it wasn't an ordinary bone, it was the bone of a human body. I asked Quincy to take me to where he found the bone. He grabbed me by the hand and led me to the very spot where he found it. "Look Gary, more dog food!" I quickly realized that there was a whole human body in there and I quickly shooed Quincy away from the scene and called Crystal River police. "Daddy, did I do something wrong?" Quincy head asked as he saw that police were surrounding where he built his sandcastle. "Of course not buddy, you've actually done a very good thing." I explained to him

Police chief Gwendolyn Jones cordoned off the area. "No one is to cross these lines, do I make myself clear?" She barked while glaring at my son. I asked the chief why she was looking at my son that way. "Because, I don't want that little runt ruining the crime scene!" She snapped back at me. I wanted to chew her face off for being so disrespectful but I knew I couldn't because she was an officer of the law and she could have me arrested at the drop of a hat. I apologized to my son and went to another part of the beach.

After taking him away from the beach because there were too many cops around, he asked me why we couldn't stay and I told him that we would come back later at some point. We toyed around Florida for a while before going out to dinner and putting Quincy to bed. "Dave, what if he has nightmares because of this sort of thing? What are we supposed to do?" She said to me as we snuggled in bed."Honeybear, I'm sure he will be fine, you worry way too much!" I said as I turned over to go to sleep. Later that night, Quincy said he's a scary woman when his eyes were shot and she was chasing after him. We were able to get him back to sleep but within the next hour he came to us again, exhibiting the same dream. We would comfort him, then he would go back to sleep, every hour on the hour he would come back to us. Finally after being totally spent, we told him to jump in bed with us. I wanted to get my freak on, but my son needed me more.

We were supposed to be in Crystal River Florida for two weeks. We shortened our vacation to two days because we thought it would be a good place for Quincy to stay. We took him to a child psychiatrist who said he might suffer from a mild case of PTSD from discovering those bones."Daddy is the mean woman going to get me? Please don't let her get me daddy!" I told him that I would always protect him and that nothing bad will ever happen to him. When we returned home, we returned home to 14 messages on our answering machine from chief Jones about the bones we had found. Chief Jones said that we needed to bring Quincy with us and come back to Florida since he is the one who discovered the bones. We asked his psychiatrist about this who strongly advised against it. Honestly though, we didn't have a choice, we didn't have a choice because we could've been arrested for obstruction of justice and we could've lost Quincy forever

"Daddy, I don't wanna go, I don't wanna see that lady again. Please don't make me go!" Margaret and I looked at each other, we really contemplated not going anywhere. But then again, the possibility of jail was just too great! I felt bad because he was three and didn't quite understand the severity of what was going on. We traveled back to Florida where we met with Gwendolyn. "Hi sweetie, my name is Gwendolyn, but you can call me Winnie. Does that sound good?" I couldn't believe the demeanor of Miss Jones. It totally changed from when we first met her. Maybe it was just a bad day or something, I'm not so sure. Quincy looked at me for approval, he looked scared but I nodded my head cream to go with her. He grabbed Chief Jones by the hand and they walked down a long hallway. We asked if we could stay in the room with Quincy; "no Mr. Anderson, we have to talk to Quincy alone. We will bring him back to you when we are finished."

As I said before, her demeanor had changed dramatically from the person we had met a couple of days before. After interviewing Quincy, they interviewed Margaret and myself. "So, do you guys know anything about the body that your son found, did you put it there?" Chief Jones snapped at us. "No, of course not! We would never kill anyone!" Margaret snapped back. They believed that and said they would call us whenever they had any leadi on the case. We went home to Stockton California and didn't hear anything for quite a while. It was actually so long that we had forgotten about the case. That is until 1993, we got a call from chief Jones with a break in the case. After all the time, the only thing they were able to determine was that the remains were of a young girl, maybe about seven or eight years old and she had been dead for about 30 years at the time of this discovery. Which means whoever it was, she was murdered sometime in 1952.

"Wait a second, we haven't heard from you in 10 years, that's all you have to give us?" I said In a snarky tone. "Yeah, we had many other cases that we had to take care of. We kind of put this one on the back burner." The problem with all this was, Quincy was now entering his teenage years and didn't remember much about the body he had found. "Dad, I've tried to put the day out of my mind for many years. Please don't rehash!" I told him I didn't want to, but we would have to go back to Florida one last time. Chief Jones wanted us to interview one last time. "But dad, why would we do that? I can't tell her any more than I told her 10 years ago. I feel bad for the family involved, but there's nothing we can do anymore!" After Quincy's second time in Crystal River Florida, we just decided to move down there.

Chief Jones had asked Quincy if there were any fragments of clothes that were on the bones so that they could examine them. "Look, Winnie, I was three years old. Do you really expect me to remember if there was….. wait a damn minute, they were fragments of a green dress on one of the bones I found. You still have the bones?" He asks. They answered yes and they took the fragments of the grass from the very place that he discovered the body 10 years prior. If you're thinking; "wait a minute, I thought they combed the whole area when they found the body." Well, they thought they did too but apparently not. Judging by the way the clothes were torn, whoever this little girl was, she was sexually assaulted.

"Sexually assaulted? How can you be so sure?" I asked chief Jones pointedly. I'm sure the chief found my question to be suspicious but I was curious as to how she came to the conclusion that she didn't just from ripped clothes. She explained that she had a special examiner examine the threads of the clothes and there were still droplets of semen on the clothes. I found this to be unbelievable, simply because the chief said that the courts have been expired for 30 years. How could semen still be on the clothes for 30 years, wouldn't it dissipate by now? I thought to myself. I didn't mention this before, but before my dad was a head football coach, before my father was A grease monkey, he was a police officer. He told me everything that I needed to know as far as police work goes, something just didn't add up.

Unfortunately, the case was in Florida and I was in California, so it really wasn't any of my concern. But yet, it was because it involved
 my son. We didn't have another breaking the case until 2000. And after this break, I had to call my parents for answers."Mr. Anderson, this is chief examiner Franklin McKay. How are you today?" I answered that I'm fine and I asked him how he was. I was eating breakfast with my family, a breakfast of waffles, bacon, and eggs. "Mr. Anderson, are you in a space where we can talk alone? I answered that I was, even though I was chowing down on my breakfast. What he said was enough to shake me to my core. "Mr. Anderson, we ran dental records and everything through every database imaginable. What I have to tell you isn't easy. But the body that your son found, the body is….. YOUR SISTER Mary Jane Anderson.

"Mr. McKay, there must be some mistake. I don't have a sister." All of this while I was trying not to choke on my waffle. Well Mr. Anderson, according to dental records, at one point you had a sister. It's her body that was found all those years ago. I called my aging parents who are now in a nursing home and I asked them about my sister. My father picked up the phone, but when I asked him about Mary Jane he paused for a second and said; "yes son, it is true, you did have a sister. She was kidnapped in 1952 and we never saw her again. Remember all those old pictures that you were asking about and we told you that they were pictures of grandma? Well, they're actually pictures of Mary Jane. We are sorry that we lied to you son, we just didn't know how to tell you!" I didn't say a word to my father that night, I hung up the phone in disbelief. I couldn't believe that my parents would like me about my own flesh and blood.

When I asked them if they tested the semen that was found on my sister's clothing, They said that they did and they told me who it was. Another beautiful shock to my system, the semen was a match for David Capelli. That's right, David motherfucking Capelli. The man that I worked for, for a number of years at his auto shop. I asked chief Jones for his address and I wanted to pay him a visit. "Mr. Anderson, with all due respect, I don't think that's such a great idea! Could damage your case. Just let the justice system take its course." I told her that I didn't want to hurt Mr. Capelli, I just wanted to talk to him about what he did. "Mr. Anderson, he'd my warning and don't talk to or touch Mr. Capelli, if you do, you will be in jail. Do I make myself clear?" I told her that I understood and that I wouldn't touch the sniveling bastard.

In 2002, they finally had enough evidence to arrest and charge a very old David Capelli. He had to be close to 90 years old. But Justice has no age limit, he killed my sister and he has to pay for what he has done. When I saw him I looked at him and said; "Mr. Capelli, it's nice to see you again. Why did you kill my sister, you fucking bastard?!" I lunged at him to attack him, I was stabbed by my son, my wife, and a lot of police officers. I was quickly detained until I could cool down. "David, don't do anything foolish, please!" My mother begged me. "Don't you dare tell me what to do, you fucking whore! You're the one who kept my sister a secret from me for many years. Don't even speak to me about what I should and shouldn't do!" I was expecting her to turn away in shame, but she whipped around and slapped me across the face.

"David Alexander Anderson, you may be a grown adult now. But you will never speak to me that way again, do I make myself clear?" I answered yes and she had to let go of my cheeks. I will tell you what, for an older woman, my mother could still pack a wallop. Listen kids, just because your mom gets older and things of that nature, doesn't mean you can mouth off to her at any point in your life. She has brought you into this world, and she will end you. Anyway, after that I never disrespected my mother in that manner again. On May 19, 2002, I found out another disturbing thing. There was a second set of semen found, it belonged to a man by the name of Anthony Delmonico. I remember Mr. Delmonico fondly. He was one of Mr. Capelli's associates at his auto shop. Although the more I thought about it, especially now, the more I began to get suspicious that Mr. Capelli wasn't running a clean auto shop. Now that I look back on it, I do think there were some extracurricular dealings going on there.

Turns out, I was right, David Capelli was a drug trafficker and child sex trafficker. He was babysitting my sister one night, August 19, 1952 (my sister was born February 19, 1944) anyway, Mr. Capelli was babysitting her and she saw something go down. Something sinister, mind you this is all coming from the memory of Mr. Capelli. She saw a murder of a man by the name of Douglas White. Douglas White was a defense attorney that was trying to get Mr. Capelli on the very charges that I just mentioned. Mr. White was getting too close so he had to die. Because my sister witnessed this murder go down, Mr. Capelli and Mr. Delmonico took my sister, killed her, drove her five hours away to Crystal River Florida from Boca Raton Florida where my family was vacationing at that time.

"I am so sorry Dave, I didn't mean to kill your sister. I was just afraid that she was going to talk to the police and I couldn't risk that." I could almost understand Not wanting to be caught by the cops, But why did they have to rape her? "Mr. Capelli, I trusted you, you were like a second father to me. Why would you do this to me, why would you do this to our family?" I was waiting for an answer, but he just turned away from me. I asked Mr. Delmonico the same thing. He just sat there in silence. "What did you do to my sister, you sick bastard! "I once again charged at them. I managed to grab Mr. Capelli by the shirt before being pulled off of him. "Yo pops, chill bro, they aren't worth it!"

I turned around quickly and saw it was my son and he was hauling my shirt. This was the first time he's ever seen me cry, I was almost 50 years old and crying like a little wussy. "Dad, it's OK, it's all going to be OK. We will get justice for aunt Mary Jane, I promise. He pulled me in close and we shared an embrace. "Thank you son, thank you so much for comforting me in my time of need." I said to him before letting go. My son was 22, but we were still extremely close which I was surprised at because normally when you're 22, you don't want to be seen with your parents. I asked Mr. Capelli and Mr. Delmonico one last time why they killed my sister and they didn't answer. I decided not to attack them this time, I decided to let Justice take its course. There were many news channels and outlets covering my sister's case. It turns out, my sister Mary Jane wasn't the only one that they had killed. It turns out that between 1942 and 1981, they killed nearly 496 children, not to mention raped them.

"Why in the hell would you do this to anyone? This is freaking inhumane!" They didn't answer me, they were arrested and charged with the murder of my sister Mary Jane. While working on my sister's case, Florida police got another call of another body that was found in Crystal River near the beach. Because technology was more advanced as to when Quincy unknowingly found my sister, they were able to determine the age and when they died a lot faster. "Dad, I'm beginning to regret finding that body. I have brought this family nothing but turmoil!" I told him not to feel bad and that he did a great thing back then. He didn't bring turmoil, he brought us closer together. "But dad, you're pissed at grandma and grandpa, what good is that?"

"Quincy, please stop worrying, this family will be fine!" In the early stages of 2003, we found that the body that was discovered at the beach yet again was another family member. The body was identified as my half sister, Ashley Gaylord. I'm finding out that I had another sister, even if it was just a half sister was astonishing. I called my dad to see if there was anything he could tell me. "Well son, I never told anyone this, not even your mother. While we were married (they married in 1943) I cheated on your mother, actually up until 1945. That's where Ashley comes in." I couldn't believe that my dad hit this from me and mom for many years. "I met a woman by the name of ester Gaylor, that's when things went awry. I didn't mean to fall in love with her but I did. I'm sorry son, I truly am!"

"Don't apologize to me dad, I apologize to the woman that you hurt and then she never knew. Go apologize to mom!" my dad was getting up there in age, "David, I can't tell your mom something like this. It would destroy our marriage!" I told him that he better figure something out, because if he didn't tell mom, I was going to. My sister Ashley was born on January 19, 1946. Examination of the body declares that she died between 1954 or 55. The results were unclear on that. Unlike the last two cases, the only evidence that was left behind of Ashley's murder was a cracked child's skull. Whoever killed her, hit her with a very blunt object. They found pieces of torn clothing on this body as well. When they tested the DNA, they discovered something very disturbing. The DNA that was found on the clothes was that of my father.

"What if my father, Mr. Capelli, and Mr. Delmonico were all in cahoots together?" I thought to myself. My father was a good man, I didn't want to think that of him but after finding out this news, what was I supposed to do or say at this point. I was beginning to see my father in a light that I wished not to see him. Could my dad be a crazy murderer? "Son, there's something you don't know about me. Mr. Capelli, Mr. Delmonico, and myself were business partners at one time. We had a murder for hire business, we didn't mean for it to start with children. It just kind of happened that way." I looked at him strangely and I said; "what the hell do you mean it just happened that way, things just don't happen that way dad, what the hell are you trying to pull?" He explained to me that it all started as taking the children as collateral for families that owed us money. When they paid us the money, we would give them back.

"Unfortunately, some parents never came up with the dough and we couldn't afford to keep them, so we had to do "damage control". I don't know where the sex with children came in, that wasn't my bag son. You have to believe me. I would never violated A child like that! " I asked him very pointedly if he participated in any of the murders. He looked away for a minute in shame, but I demanded an answer."Yes David, unfortunately, I did participate in one and it made me sick to my core. It was your sister Mary Jane's murder. You see son, we were very poor and I had to borrow money from Mr. Capelli for groceries and other things so we could have a halfway decent life. When I couldn't pay him back, he forced me to kill Mary Jane. I didn't want to, but she blackmailed me Into doing it. He blackmailed me into it by threatening to tell your mother about my sexual conquests that I committed behind her back. I couldn't let that happen, I couldn't let it destroy the fabric of our family. But yet, I myself destroyed the very fabric I was trying to protect.

"Wait a minute, you killed our daughter? How could you do that, how could you do that to this family?!" When my father turned around, he realized that my mother was standing right there. She looked pissed and she had tears in her eyes. "Marty I don't believe you, I don't believe that you destroyed the fabric of this family. I beat myself up for many years because I thought maybe I should've kept it better on her. But then I found out it was you, it's your fault!" my mother walked away and a half and I went after her. "Momma, please calm down, dad's an old fool. You were much better off without him, he doesn't deserve a woman like you." She looked at me and she said: "thanks David, I'm glad I have such a sweet son like you. We've been married for 60 years, come to find out we have 60 years of secrets. I don't know if I can ever trust your father again!"

"I love your father David, I really do. But what he has done to this family is unforgivable. I'm thinking about filing for divorce. It's not that I want to, it's that I feel that I have to." As I said before son, I don't think I can trust your father again." I begged my mother to reconsider. However, her mind was made up and there was nothing any of us could do or say to change her mind. She told my father, needless to say he was not happy. "Divorce, divorce?! How could you divorce me after all the time we spent together Marla. You must not love me anymore." My mother said that was untrue, but the fact that he kept a secret from her made her not trust him. My father said that he understood, but begged her to give him another chance. She refused."

After 60 years of marriage, my mother filed for divorce from my father. Even though I was now 50 years old, it still hurt me a tiny bit. It hurt me because I thought back to the time where I cheated on Margaret with Reshma and how it almost ended my family. I hated the thought of it happening to my parents, especially after 60 years."Marla please reconsider, baby I love you!" My father begged my mother as she was packing her bags. "You love me, you love me! A person who loves someone doesn't hide a secret from them for more than 60 years. Don't tell me you love me, because you don't mean it!" Did I forget to mention that my mother and father had moved to Crystal River Florida shortly after 1997? If I did I'm sorry, but yes, my parents moved to Crystal River Florida in 1997 after my dad retired from the grease monkey business.

After finding out that his grandparents divorced, Quincy slipped into a deep depression and struggled with it for many years. He struggled with depression until the early part of 2005, that is when he took a shotgun and blew his brains out. He felt so guilty about finding that body and thinking that he destroyed our family, he just killed himself. Capelli and Delmonico were entering the part of old age where they were starting to get senile. They brought them to trial, but many people argued that it wouldn't do any good because anything that they say could be chopped up to dementia. "Mrs. Anderson, are you sure you want to proceed with this trial, after all they are getting older!" Our attorney Norman Greenbaum had asked. "Of course Mr. Greenbaum, Of course I want to proceed with the trial, they've done something wrong and they need to be punished for it. I don't care if one of them is my husband or ox-husband I should say, and I don't care how old they are."

One day, I was sitting with my dad drinking a cup of coffee and a loud pound echoed across the front door. When I opened the door, two uniformed police officers entered my home. "Are you Martin and Anderson sir?" One of the officers asked. I answered no and pointed to the living room. I heard a scuffle going on and when I went into the living room, I saw that they had my father on the floor trying to apprehend him. "What is the meaning of this? I didn't do anything wrong, let me up right this minute!" My father looked at me for help, but I ignored him, almost as if he wasn't there. "Son, please, help me. I'm sorry for what I've done in my life, but I do not deserve this type of brutality!"

I ignored him again and they took him away in handcuffs. "Son, son, son, please! Help me get out of this. You know I love you!" I would visit him in jail almost every day, I was still pissed at him, but he was my father after all. Mom on the other hand, well mom, didn't forgive him so easily. Who could blame her? As we were preparing to bring them to trial in early 2006. My father passed away at age 84. (Born sometime in 1922). "You see Mrs. Anderson, this is why I wanted the trial to be forgotten about. These guys are way too old, they will be dead before we even start these trials. My mother was a bit of a hard ass and didn't care. She said that she wanted the people who hurt her family prosecuted to the fullest extent of the law.

During that time, I decided to train for the police academy. I wanted to handle these cases myself and make sure everything was done right. Everything under the sun to protect my family's name. I graduated from the police academy in the latter part of 2006 and started on foot patrol. I hated this, I wanted to get my feet deep in the dirt or sand it so to speak of my family's case. "Chief, can I talk to you for a second? It's really important. She motioned to me inside and offered me a seat, and a drink. I sat down and I had a soda."Chief, as you know, the Anderson case is really important to me and personal. Please put me on this freaking case!" Chief Jones (Shalonda Jones who is Gwendolyn's daughter). She leaned back in her chair and pondered a thought for a moment. "Look, Anderson, I know this is important to you. However, I can't put you on the case. Your emotions would get in the way too much, and we can't have that. Especially because you're a rookie on the police force, I'm sorry Anderson, but the answer is no."

I was upset, but I understood. I know what you're thinking; "you're 50 some years old, why would you want to go chasing after criminals now?" This was my family God dammit, I had to do whatever it took to protect them. I couldn't let my last name be soiled because of something stupid that my father did years ago. Against chief Jones' wishes, I snuck into the forensic files Da Dip with this case instead of examining them. As I was searching through the files, I learned something shocking. Marty Anderson wasn't my father, My father was Mr. Capelli. My mother married him in 1941 according to the records. Only to divorce in many the man who I knew as my father two years later. They apparently hooked back up in March of 1953 and conceived me after my father had been away visiting family for a funeral in Austin Texas.

"You just couldn't leave well enough alone, could you son?" When I turned around, my mother was standing in the doorway of the file room. "Momma, what are you doing here?" I asked, trying not to shit my pants from being scared so much. "Yes, yes David, I had an affair. I'm not proud of it but it happened. I'm also not proud of what I'm about to do." She pulled out a gun and waved me against the wall. "Mama, please mama, please don't do this! "I begged her. "Shut up Dave, get up against the wall and do exactly as I say!"

"OK mama, okay, let's just calm down and talk about this. No one needs to die today, remember all the fun times we had?" She slammed the gun against the wall and told me to be quiet. I quickly shut my mouth and let her say her piece. "You know something, your father didn't kill all those people, I did! That's right son, it was me. At first it was just an accident, then I got a taste of the bloodlust and I could not control myself. I didn't mean to kill my children, it just happened. During the time it all went down, they would never believe that a woman did any of this so your father or what you assumed to be your father, took the fall for me and Mr. Capelli."

"I'm sorry son, but now you know too much. I must kill you now!" As soon as she clicked the chamber, she was tackled by three uniformed police officers. I quickly said thank you to them and left the room. After leaving the room, I got in my car, I took a long drive and contemplated everything that I just witnessed. "My mother was a murderer, not my father, my mother. How in the world do you deal with that?" I thought to myself. One night Margaret and I were laying in bed and I said; "babe, what would you do if you were in this situation. What would you do if you found out that your mother was a cold-blooded murderer?" She looked at me and she shook her shoulders; "Dave, I don't know what I would do, I know that you don't want to see your mother in handcuffs, but you also need to do the right thing because you are an officer of the wall. I knew she was right. It was just that my mother was aging and I didn't want to see her spend the rest of her life in jail.

I went to visit her a couple days later. "David, I'm sorry for trying to kill you, I'm a bad person and I should've never been in the general population. I asked her about the sexual assaults with the children. "Honestly son, I have no idea about that. That was not my portion of the deal, that was more of your father's and Mr. Delmonico's deal. Maybe they were just sick perverts, I really don't know. I had asked why she killed my sisters and I wanted the truth. "Well son, you might want to sit down with us. You see, there's something your Mari didn't tell you, your sisters were mentally retarded. During that time, we didn't know exactly what to do with children like that. We didn't want to have the constant responsibility of doctors appointments, and things that came with having a disabled child.

I nearly felt sick to my stomach. "So you killed my sisters, because they were mentally retarded? Momma, how could you?" She told me that it wasn't an easy decision but back in those times, she felt that it was something that had to be done. "No mama, no it didn't need to be done, you chose to do it. You know what, I hope you rot in hell for the rest of your life for what you have done, you do not deserve to see the light of day!`` She looked down at the floor and then two armed guards let her back to her cell. Before she left, she stood up and she said; "I just want you to know son, I'm sorry!"" I turned away from her and didn't acknowledge her existence. I couldn't believe that my mother was that selfish.

I couldn't believe that the Life I had built for almost 60 years was a total lie. In 2007 at the age of 54, I became chief of Crystal River Florida police. This was after Shalonda Jones had died in an unfortunate car accident. In 2008, my mother went to trial. The judge on the docket was Henry Barnett. Henry Barnett had been on the bench for 30 years. Judge Barnett asked my mother how she pleaded. She said that she pleaded not guilty. Hearing that I asked her; "how can you tell me what you told me, and then turned around and played the guilty?" I stormed off because I was upset.

My mother rotted away in jail for the next two years. "Son, I've done a lot of wrong things in my life, and I do mean a lot. However, the one thing I did right in life was raising you. I'm sorry things had to turn out this way, I'm just so so sorry." On August 19, 2009, my mother went in front of Judge Barnett. "Mrs. Anderson, you stand accused of the murders of Mary Jane Anderson and Ashley Gaylor. Do you still plead not guilty?" She looked down at the floor for a second, then she looked back up at Judge Barnett.``Yes your honor, still not guilty!" I hired an attorney for the name of Brian Nicholson. He was the first to cross examine my mother. "Mrs. Anderson, is it true that you admitted to your son that you killed your two daughters because both of them ended up mentally retarded. Is that true at all Mrs. Anderson? She swallowed hard, looking down at the floor but she said; it is true Mr. Nicholson, indeed, it is true. But I didn't know what else to do, what was I supposed to do with two mentally challenged kids in the 1940s and some of the 1950s?" I should make it a point to mention that they were going to bring Mr. Capelli and Mr. Delmonico to trial as well but they died earlier that year at the ages of 94 and 90 respectively.

"Mrs. Anderson, that is no excuse for what you did." I couldn't believe that my mother tried to defend her actions. Well, I mean I'm not exactly sure what I would've done in the 1940s and 50s with two mentally retarded kids, but I can assure you that I would not have killed them. Or let somebody have sex with their life with bodies like some sort of pervert. My mother barely looked at me during the trial. Surprisingly enough, the juries were deadlocked. I couldn't imagine why, my mother was obviously very sick in the head and deserved to be in jail. Although, maybe they feel bad because she was aging. I didn't care that my mother was aging, I didn't care that she may only spend a month in jail before she fucking dies. I just wanted justice to be served.

Her attorney argued or at least tried to argue that her actions give me the time frame of when it happened were totally justified. I stood up in the quart room and I said; "justified? Justified? How do you justify taking two innocent lives? Those were my sisters, I never got to meet them because my mother killed them. I never got to build a relationship with them, because they were taken away too soon. How do you justify that counselor?" I knew that her attorney would try to get her off due to age related problems. My mother was starting to develop dementia, arthritis, you name it she had it. Again, I did feel bad for my mother but she needed to learn her lesson.

Three years go by and she is sitting in jail, still waiting for a sentencing. "Ma'am, it's time. They said to her as they let her out of her jail cell. I know this because they let me walk with her to the room where she would receive her sentencing. I never saw that woman look so scared in her life, I almost felt bad for her. Notice I say almost, because as soon as I feel bad for what she did, I remembered exactly what she did and any sympathy I had went away. "Momma, is there anything else you want to say to me or to your daughters in heaven?" I asked her as we walked down the dark, long and damp hallway. She shook her head no and I grabbed her hand as we walked further down the hallway.

I held her hand because even though she was a monster in my eyes, I felt like she needed some sort of comfort. I'm her son, I'm supposed to provide that comfort. I didn't want to, but I felt obligated to. "David, please don't let them send me up the river. I'm too old, I'm too fragile, I'm too sick. I don't want to go to jail, if I would've known that this was the consequences of my actions all those years ago, I would never have done any of this. I thought since I had gotten away with it for so long, I thought that it was all behind me. But you just had to snoop around and dig up all this old shit, didn't you?" I quickly let go of her hand after she said that to me. She clearly had no remorse for what she had done, even though she had said that she did.

"All rise. The Honorable Judge Barnett presiding." Said the bailiff. My heart skipped a beat, and everything slowed down as I watched the judge walk across the podium to his chair. "Counselor Davis, do you have any closing arguments?" Geraldine Davis was my mother's attorney, you know the one that said it was acceptable for her to kill my sisters? Yeah, that bitch! I hated her because she tried to condone what my mother did. But she said that she had no closing arguments. They asked my attorney if he had any closing arguments or statements. When they both said no, we were able to continue the trial.

"Miss Anderson, for the murders of Ashley Gaylor and Mary Jane Anderson, May God have mercy on your soul. What you did, regardless of the timeline, was pure and utter evil. "Jury, have you reached a verdict?" Juror number 64 Juanita Lopez read the verdict. "We the jury, in the state of Florida, found the defendant, Marla Anderson……. GUILTY!" The way that the judge looked at my mother after the verdict was red, I knew it couldn't be good."Miss Anderson, you have been found guilty on all charges. Do you have anything to say for yourself?" She shook her head no and stood there awaiting her fate.

"Miss Anderson, I sent them to you to two consecutive life sentences for the murders you have committed. I really hope you enjoyed the sunlight for all those years, and all the trips to the beach that you had over the years, because you will never ever see the lighter day again! "She looked scared, her voice shook and she said: "two life sentences? Two of them? Your Honor, don't you think that's a little extreme?" she said no sharply, slammed her Gavel, and the sentence was finalized. At the age of 89, on August 19, 2012, she motioned or tried to motion for another trial. But she failed. Despite what I thought about my mother now, Visited her in jail until her death on July 3, 2021 at age 98. She never grew tired of telling me how sorry she was for what she did. She finally realized how much of a monster she truly was, she finally realized that she deserved to be in jail. I miss my mother terribly, but she needed to be taught a valuable lesson and I think jail really helped her with that.